# Bold Springtime to Color

Eleri Fowler

# to Color

## Eleri Fowler

**HARPER**

*An Imprint of HarperCollinsPublishers*

For J.B., our precious
little springtime bloom.
Can't wait to watch you
blossom.

x

—E.F.

Bold Springtime to Color
By Eleri Fowler
Copyright © 2017 by HarperCollins Publishers
All rights reserved. Printed in the United States of America.
No part of this book may be used or reproduced in any manner whatsoever without written
permission except in the case of brief quotations embodied in critical articles and reviews.
For information address HarperCollins Children's Books,
a division of HarperCollins Publishers, 195 Broadway, New York, NY 10007.
www.harpercollinschildrens.com

ISBN 978-0-06-256996-7

The artist used pencil, paper, brush pens, fineliner pen, and computer to create
the illustrations for this book.
Interior hand lettering by Trina Dalziel
Cover hand lettering by Eleri Fowler
Typography by Whitney Manger

17  18  19  20  21    PC/LSCW    10  9  8  7  6  5  4  3  2  1
❖
First Edition

This book belongs to

_____

This book is a window into
my sketchbook: brimming with the
wonderful images of springtime that lift my spirit
no matter what the season. You'll find designs featuring
inspirational quotes, plus flowers, rain boots, ladybugs,
birdhouses, and more—all ready for you to make your own!
There are so many creative ways to enjoy this book. The choice is yours—
experiment with colored pencils, gel pens, or felt-tip pens. Do try a few test
doodles to make sure your pens don't bleed through the paper! If you are using
colored pencils, try building up different shades and tones of color within your
design. This will add depth and mimic the variety of different colors that exist in
nature. The best way I've found to mix two or more colors together is to layer each
color in turn from lightest to darkest. That way, you can control the intensity
of the color. If you're feeling a bit daring, try using watercolors! (But be sure
to let them dry before turning the page.) Once you've filled your pages
with glorious color, why stop there? You can be sure I won't be limited
to just coloring—my copy of the book will be bursting with little
embellishments like gems, sequins, and glitter. Be creative!
I love that no two finished books will look alike:
embrace that! The most important thing is to
experiment and have fun.

*Eleri*

# My Influences

Nature has a massive influence on my work. I love to go on long walks in the country and along the coast. My area of Wales is bursting with beautiful gardens and rolling hills, which means inspiration is just outside my front door!

The abundance of nature, the animals, and breathtaking scenery cannot fail to fill your imagination. I always make sure that I have a sketchbook and laptop on hand to start the next project wherever inspiration strikes. Spending time outdoors walking and sketching always makes me feel extra energized and full of creativity!

# Behind the Scenes:
## How I Create My Art to Color

I always start a project with a simple sketch using a mechanical pencil. I am a bit of a perfectionist, so one of my favorite tools in the world is my 0.35mm pencil, as it gives such a smooth, precise line. I like to work on layout paper as it is semitransparent, which is great for tracing. Perhaps I'm a bit old-fashioned, but I like to stick to traditional drawing methods as much as possible and only use the computer for final tweaks for print.

To create my illustrations, first I'll sketch out a rough shape—laying out the main elements in the piece. Then I'll trace over it, adding in more details. I'll repeat this stage a few times until I end up with a piece that I am happy with. Then, I redraw the final image using a black fineliner pen (0.05 is my preference as, just like with my pencil, it gives a very thin and accurate line).

The robin
and his mate
FLEW
backward and forward
like tiny
STREAKS of LIGHTNING.

—Frances Hodgson Burnett

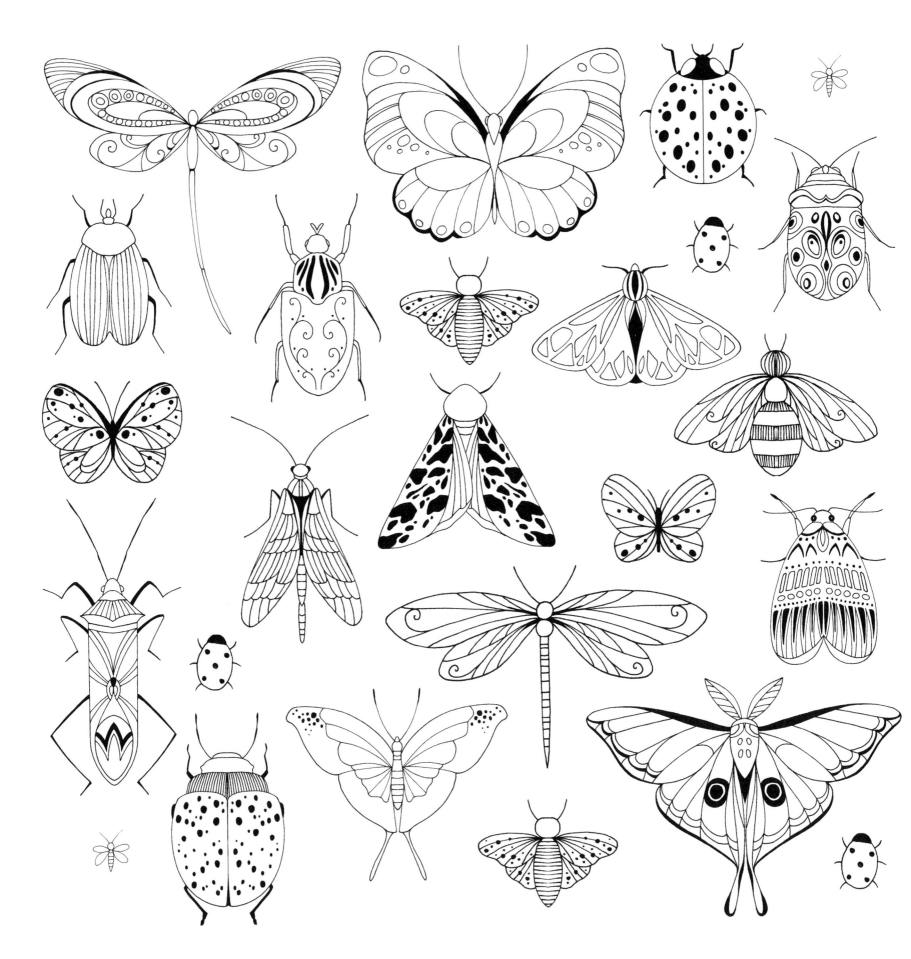

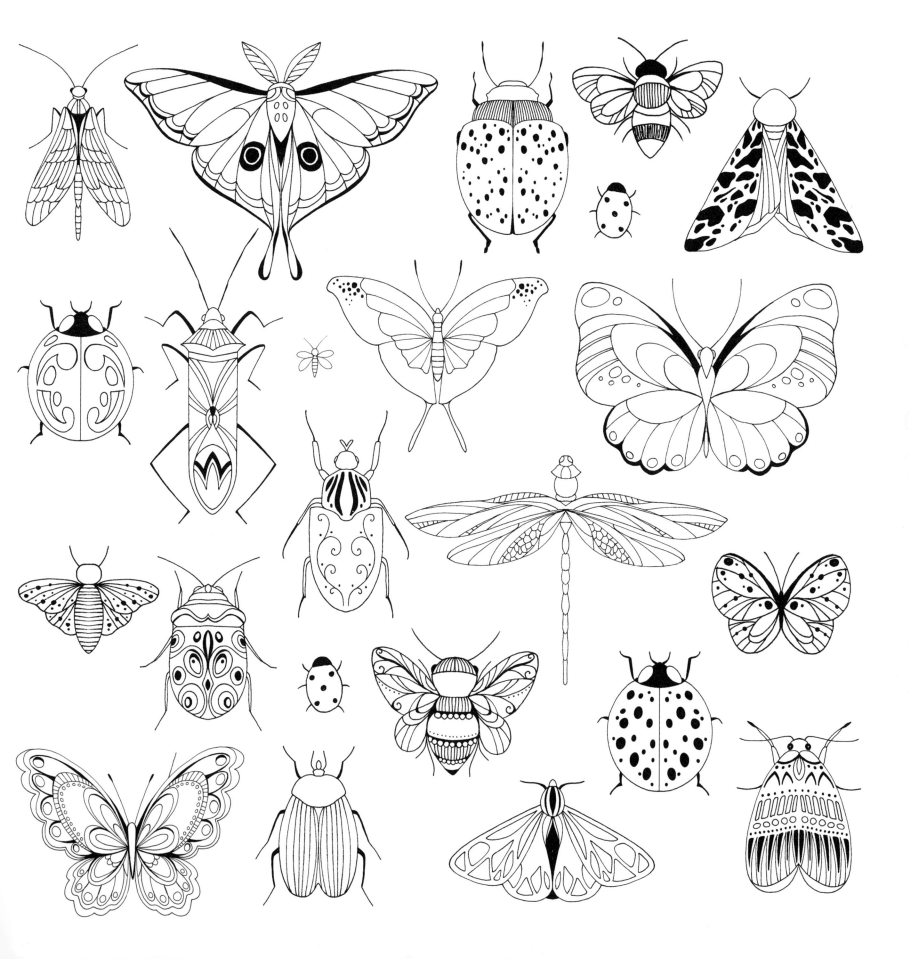

HELLO, SPRING

Sweet spring,
full of sweet days
and
roses
—George Herbert

I sing
of brooks,
of blossoms,
birds,
and bowers.

—Robert Herrick

Nature GIVES TO EVERY time and season some beauties of its own.

—Charles Dickens

On wings
of
SONG

—Heinrich Heine

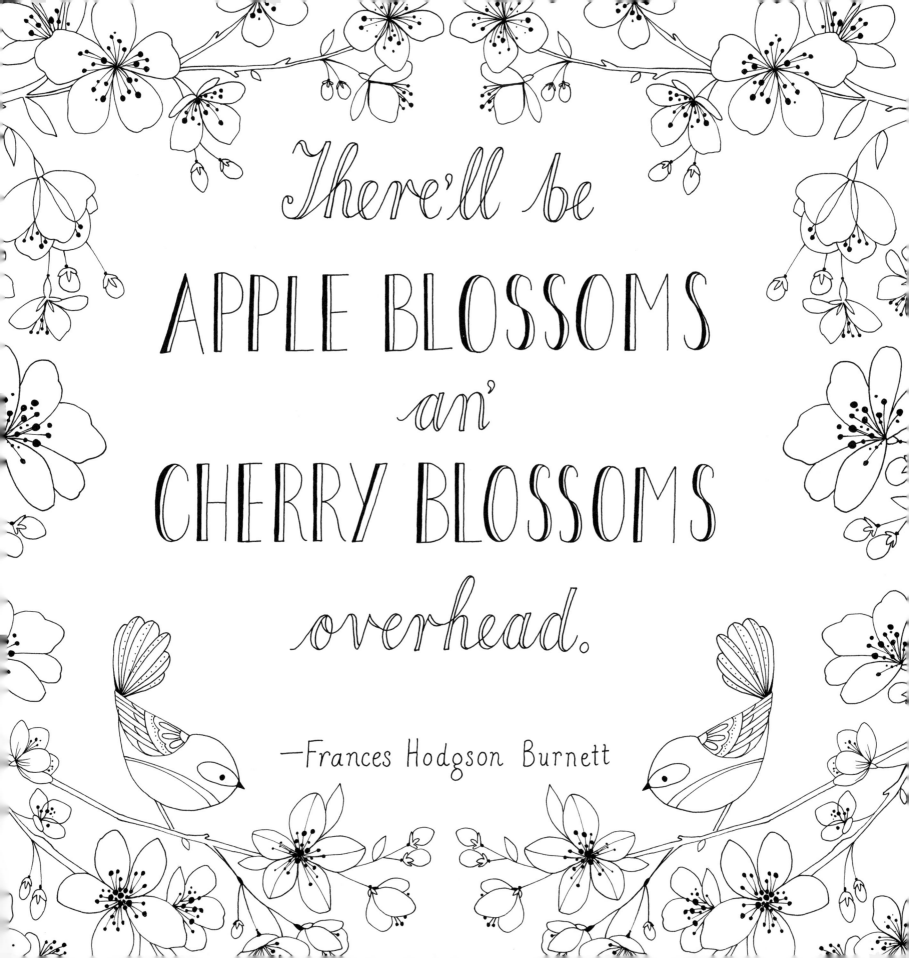

There'll be
APPLE BLOSSOMS
an'
CHERRY BLOSSOMS
overhead.

—Frances Hodgson Burnett

Swims
the world in
ecstasy,
THE FOREST WAVES,
the morning breaks,
THE PASTURES SLEEP,
ripple the lakes.

—Ralph Waldo Emerson

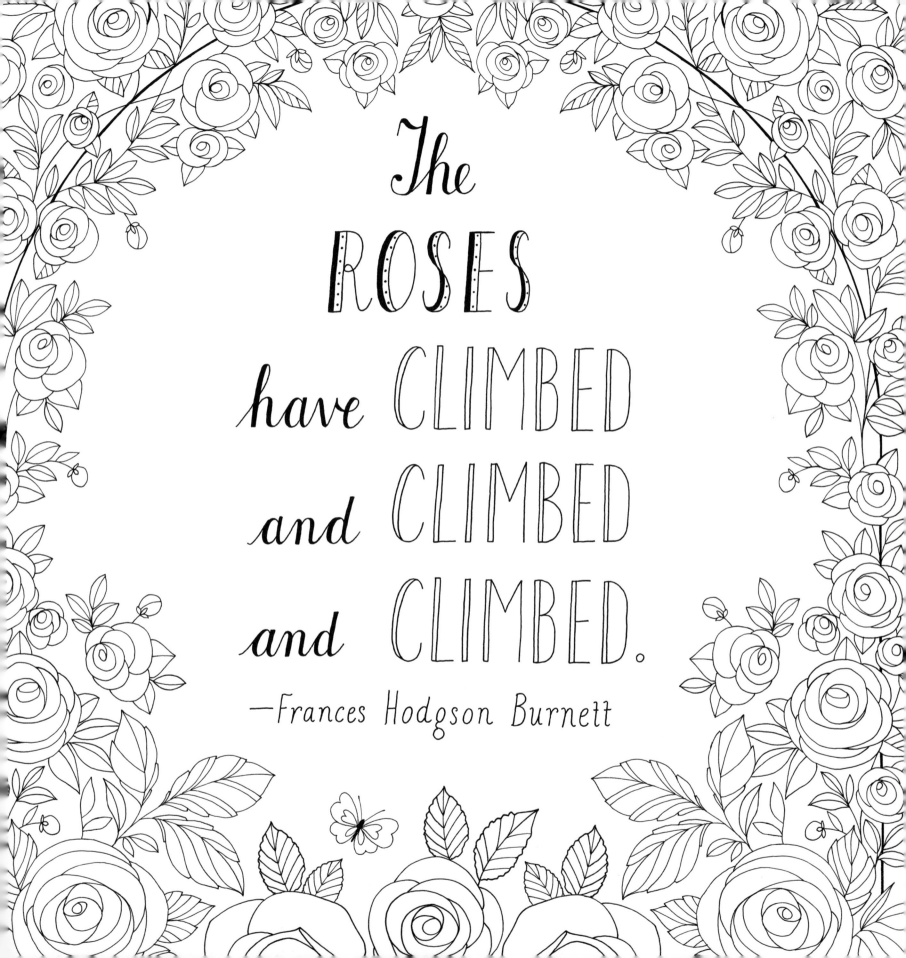

The
ROSES
have CLIMBED
and CLIMBED
and CLIMBED.
—Frances Hodgson Burnett

BLOOM

All at once
I SAW A CROWD,
A host,
of
GOLDEN DAFFODILS.

—William Wordsworth

STRAWBERRIES

The first SPARROW of SPRING!

—Henry D. Thoreau

Can words DESCRIBE the FRAGRANCE of the VERY BREATH of spring?

—Neltje Blanchan

SPRING

*is*

THE TIME OF

*plans and projects.*

—Leo Tolstoy

THE
SUN
JUST TOUCHED
the morning.

—Emily Dickinson

There are
FLOWERS uncurling
and BUDS
on everything.

—Frances Hodgson Burnett

Earth LAUGHS in flowers.

—Ralph Waldo Emerson

I HAVE come from the spring-woods.

—Ralph Waldo Emerson

It is here
NOW!
It has come,
the Spring!

—Frances Hodgson Burnett

Sing, ROBIN, sing

—Christina Rossetti

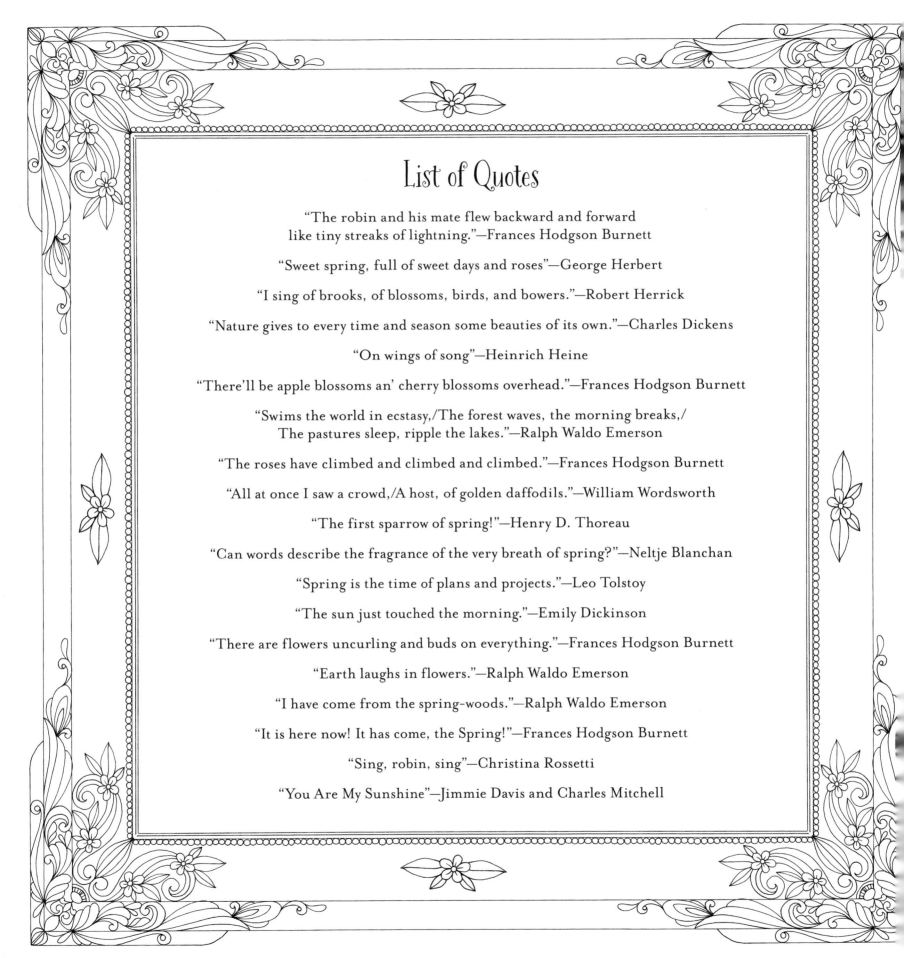

# List of Quotes

"The robin and his mate flew backward and forward
like tiny streaks of lightning."—Frances Hodgson Burnett

"Sweet spring, full of sweet days and roses"—George Herbert

"I sing of brooks, of blossoms, birds, and bowers."—Robert Herrick

"Nature gives to every time and season some beauties of its own."—Charles Dickens

"On wings of song"—Heinrich Heine

"There'll be apple blossoms an' cherry blossoms overhead."—Frances Hodgson Burnett

"Swims the world in ecstasy,/The forest waves, the morning breaks,/
The pastures sleep, ripple the lakes."—Ralph Waldo Emerson

"The roses have climbed and climbed and climbed."—Frances Hodgson Burnett

"All at once I saw a crowd,/A host, of golden daffodils."—William Wordsworth

"The first sparrow of spring!"—Henry D. Thoreau

"Can words describe the fragrance of the very breath of spring?"—Neltje Blanchan

"Spring is the time of plans and projects."—Leo Tolstoy

"The sun just touched the morning."—Emily Dickinson

"There are flowers uncurling and buds on everything."—Frances Hodgson Burnett

"Earth laughs in flowers."—Ralph Waldo Emerson

"I have come from the spring-woods."—Ralph Waldo Emerson

"It is here now! It has come, the Spring!"—Frances Hodgson Burnett

"Sing, robin, sing"—Christina Rossetti

"You Are My Sunshine"—Jimmie Davis and Charles Mitchell